# The Hair of Zoe

## Fleefenbacher Goes to School

LAURIE
HALSE
ANDERSON

ILLUSTRATED BY ARD HOYT

Atheneum Books for Young Readers

New York   London   Toronto   Sydney   New Delhi

**ZOE FLEEFENBACHER**
had one blue eye and one green eye,
and bright red hair that went on . . .

. . . forever.

When Zoe was a baby, she needed two strollers
and two cribs and two high chairs. One for
Zoe Fleefenbacher and one for Zoe's hair.

When she was two years old, Zoe's hair learned how to open the cookie jar.

At three, her hair could turn on the TV, pour a glass of juice, pet the cat, and play on the computer—all at the same time.

At four, it learned to fly.

Mom and Dad Fleefenbacher threw out the brushes and combs. The hair of their Zoe was wild and beautiful.

It was her sail, her kite, her flag.

Zoe had Mrs. Brodhag for kindergarten.

Mrs. Brodhag let Zoe's hair pick up the trash,
erase the board, and set the table for snack.
At nap time, the hair was a comfort.

Zoe had Ms. Trisk for first grade.
Ms. Trisk didn't fool around.

"School has rules," she said.
"No wild hair in my class!"

Zoe Fleefenbacher's hair did not
listen. When Ms. Trisk wrote
on the board, Zoe's hair tickled
everybody.

Ms. Trisk sat Zoe in time-out.
Zoe's hair drew all over the walls.

Ms. Trisk took charge of the situation.

Big mistake.

"This must stop!" shouted Ms. Trisk.

"School has rules!"

Ms. Trisk demanded a meeting with *the principal*. Zoe's hair had to wait outside.

The grown-ups agreed. School had rules. That hair had to be tamed.

Zoe tried a ponytail.

It didn't work.

Zoe tried braids.

No good.

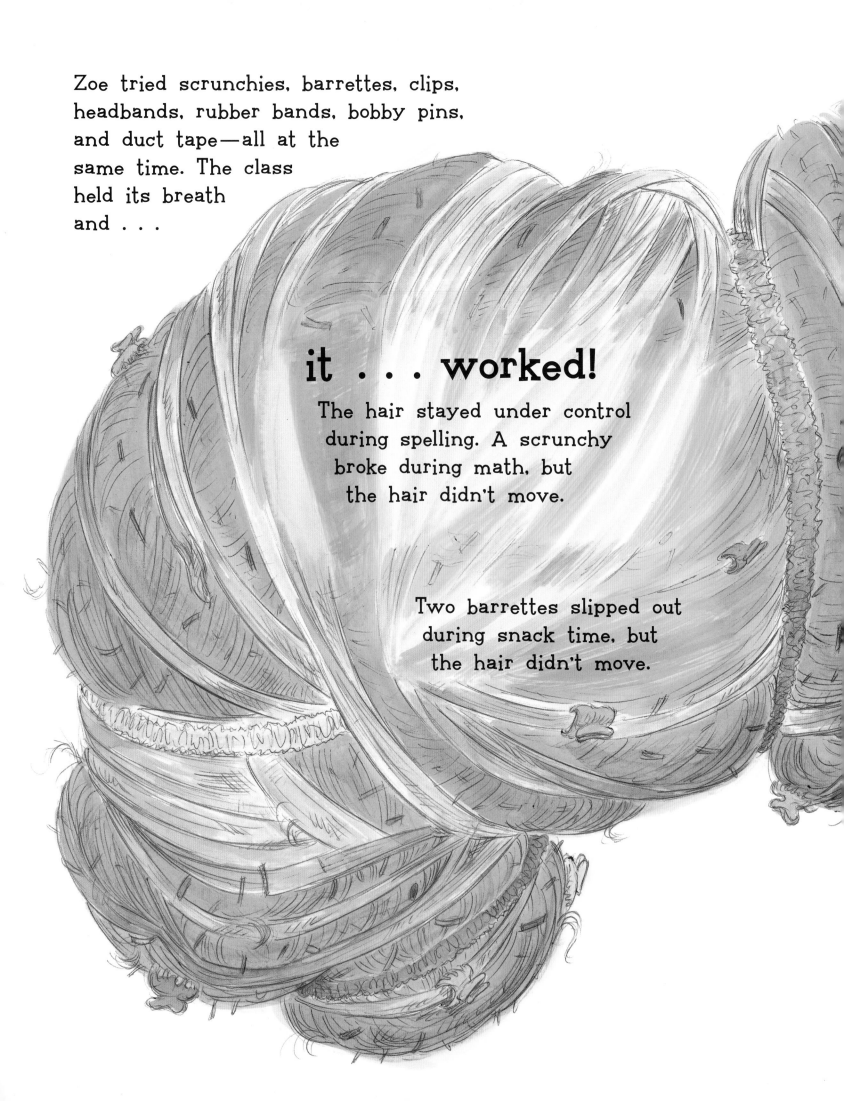

Zoe tried scrunchies, barrettes, clips, headbands, rubber bands, bobby pins, and duct tape—all at the same time. The class held its breath and . . .

## it . . . worked!

The hair stayed under control during spelling. A scrunchy broke during math, but the hair didn't move.

Two barrettes slipped out during snack time, but the hair didn't move.

"First grade has rules," Ms. Trisk reminded the class. And then she smiled.

Zoe couldn't smile. It felt like all the rules in the world were sitting on top of her head.

Ms. Trisk started the science lesson. She held up a ball. "This is the Sun." She held up another ball. "Mercury orbits the Sun." She picked up three other balls. "This is Venus, Mars, and here is the Earth."

She dropped the Earth. The class giggled.

"First grade has rules," Ms. Trisk reminded them. "No giggling."

Zoe lifted her head off the desk.
A bobby pin fell to the floor.
One red strand of hair unfurled.

Ms. Trisk picked up two more balls. "Pretend that these are Jupiter and Saturn and that all the planets are spinning and orbiting around the Sun."
**BAM! BAM! BAM!**
Jupiter, Mars, and Venus fell to the floor and rolled into the corner.

**Ping! Ping! Ping!**
Bobby pins rained on the floor around Zoe.

"Oh, my," said Ms. Trisk.

**Snap! Snap!** Rubber bands and scrunchies bounced off the ceiling. Barrettes, headbands, and duct tape rocketed through the air. The hair of Zoe Fleefenbacher exploded into the classroom.

"I can help!" Zoe hollered. "I know how to do it!"

Whap! Pop! Whoosh!

The class gasped. Zoe's hair was loose!
The kids grabbed their crayons and hid their
scissors. Ms. Trisk dived for the gerbils' cage.

Zoe smoothed her hair and raised her hand. "Please, Ms. Trisk," she said. "I want to help. Can I try?"

Ms. Trisk nodded.

Zoe's hair picked up Mercury, Venus, the Earth, Mars, Jupiter, Saturn, Uranus, Neptune, and the Sun.

SUN

"The planets spin . . . ," said Ms. Trisk.

Zoe's hair spun the planets.

". . . as they orbit the Sun."

Zoe's hair twirled the planets along their paths.

That day the first-grade students in Ms. Trisk's room learned all about the planets.

Ms. Trisk learned some things too.

"My goodness," said Ms. Trisk. "That is some amazing hair. That's helpful hair! That's handy hair!"

Zoe Fleefenbacher had one blue eye and one green eye, and handy, helpful, amazing hair . . .

that
found
a place
in first
grade.

This book is dedicated to my daughter,
Meredith Anderson, for being an energetic student
and becoming an understanding teacher.—L. H. A.

To my Grandmother LaPreal, with eternal gratitude for
sharing your love, your home, your stories, and your
nose with me—but most of all for being my friend.
Always your Arizona cowboy—A. H.

ACKNOWLEDGMENTS
I would like to jump up and down and shout "THANK YOU" to the enthusiastic
crew of rule-benders who helped bring Zoe to life: artist, Ard Hoyt; book
designer, Jessica Handelman; and our irrepressible editor, Kevin Lewis.—L. H. A.

A
atheneum

ATHENEUM BOOKS FOR YOUNG READERS
An imprint of Simon & Schuster Children's Publishing Division
1230 Avenue of the Americas, New York, New York 10020
Text copyright © 2009 by Laurie Halse Anderson • Illustrations copyright © 2009 by Ard Hoyt
All rights reserved, including the right of reproduction in whole or in part in any form.
ATHENEUM BOOKS FOR YOUNG READERS is a registered trademark of Simon & Schuster, Inc.
Atheneum logo is a trademark of Simon & Schuster, Inc.
For information about special discounts for bulk purchases, please contact Simon & Schuster Special Sales at
1-866-506-1949 or business@simonandschuster.com.
The Simon & Schuster Speakers Bureau can bring authors to your live event. For more information or to book
an event, contact the Simon & Schuster Speakers Bureau at 1-866-248-3049 or
visit our website at www.simonspeakers.com.
Also available in a Simon & Schuster Books for Young Readers hardcover edition
Book design by Jessica Handelman • The text for this book was set in Plumbsky.
The illustrations for this book were rendered in pen and ink with watercolor on Arches paper.
Manufactured in China • 0519 SCP
First Atheneum Books for Young Readers paperback edition June 2019
2  4  6  8  10  9  7  5  3
The Library of Congress has cataloged the hardcover edition as follows:
Anderson, Laurie Halse. • The hair of Zoe Fleefenbacher goes to school / Laurie Halse Anderson ; illustrated
by Ard Hoyt–1st ed. • p. cm. • Summary: A little girl's talented and untamed hair can open cookie jars and
play computer games, much to the displeasure of her strict first-grade teacher who has rules for everything,
including hair. • ISBN 978-0-689-85809-3 (hc) • ISBN 978-1-5344-5226-8 (pbk) • ISBN 978-1-4424-4509-3
(eBook) [1. Hair–Fiction. 2. Rules (Philosophy)–Fiction. 3. Schools–Fiction. 4. Humorous stories.] I. Hoyt, Ard, ill.
II. Title. • PZ7.A54385Hai 2009 • [E]–dc22  2007045161